DUDLEY PUBLIC LIBRARIES

The loan of this book may be renewed if not required by other readers, by contacting the library from which it was borrowed.

CP/494

More great reads in the SHADES 2.0 series:

SHADES 2.0

MAU MAU BROTHER

Tish Farrell

Ransom

SHADES 2.0
Mau Mau Brother
by Tish Farrell

Published by Ransom Publishing Ltd.
Radley House, 8 St. Cross Road, Winchester, Hampshire SO23 9HX, UK
www.ransom.co.uk

ISBN   978 178127 630 3
First published in 2014

CONTENTS

ONE

Conflict

This is the story of my war – the war that made me hate my own big brother.

My name is Thuo. I am fifteen years old, and the time is 1955. In Kenya the British have ruled us for sixty years, but now the freedom fighters have gone to their forest strongholds.

They are fighting to take our land back.

Everywhere people whisper 'Mau Mau'.
Everywhere there is suspicion. Here in the
Native Reserve, we wonder which neighbour is
Mau Mau and which a British informer.

Every day I am afraid. Even in my sleep I
tremble.

Some days the British planes bomb the
forest near the Reserve. Some days platoons of
British soldiers sweep across the hills searching
for the freedom fighters, firing their guns at
people who look like me. Sometimes the
African Home Guards swoop and search our
homes.

Sometimes the freedom fighters come out of
the forest, quietly as ghosts, and force us to
swear oaths to help them.

But it is not the British I hate most, nor the
Home Guards who beat up my father and sent
him to Manyani detention camp.

No. It is Kungu I hate.

Once I was proud of him: when he put on

the sergeant's uniform and went off to fight for King George in the King's African Rifles. The KAR helped Britain defeat the Japanese in Burma. They came home heroes.

But then Kungu grew angry. He said the British officers had promised the African soldiers land, but after the war they forgot their promise.

And so one day Kungu left the Reserve. He went to the forest on God's Mountain and joined the Land and Freedom Army that the British call Mau Mau.

He said he would fight to end British rule.

And that is how Kungu wrecked our lives, making war with the British.

Now Kungu haunts my dreams, mocking my terror. He knows I am a coward, and so I hate him.

And I will have no peace until my brother is dead.

TWO

Bombers

On the day we lose our home, my little brother Mugo and I are taking the goats to pasture.

It is January, high summer. All around, doves coo and cornstalks rustle, and I think: *how can there be war on so fine a day?*

The sun is just rising and Mugo runs ahead, slapping dew from the grasses, so the drops fly like jewels through the sky. I remember doing that too, when I was younger.

But I was not minding goats. I was hurrying to school, wearing the white shirt, bought four sizes too big from the Indian trader so it will last for years. And I am wearing khaki shorts instead of my kidskin wrap. It is my first day at the Kikuyu Independent School.

Father has taken me away from the Scottish Mission, saying the teachers there teach Africans to be nothing better than clerks and house servants. He says I will have a better future at KIS.

I don't. With the uprising, the British close my school. I have been minding goats ever since. It is another reason to hate Kungu.

Mugo goes on swishing grasses, but I am so busy fuming I do not hear planes. Then the world shakes to bits.

Boom-boom-ker-boom.

Mugo jumps like a spooked deer. And we run. At the top of the ridge we see the Lincoln

bombers like giant birds above the forest.
Down come the bombs. One, two … five, more
… till I want to vomit. The hills sprout
volcanoes. Trees fly apart. Our goats shriek.

We stand and stare as if turned to stone.
The bombers do not target our farms, only the
forests outside the Reserve.

When the planes drone away and the smoke
clears, we stare at God's Mountain. The
jagged snow peaks, the dark forest slopes, are
still there. It is hard to believe.

'Kungu?' Mugo's eyes dart round in case
there's anyone to hear. 'They have killed him?'
he mouths. My stomach churns. I glance
round too, but say nothing. I do not yell, 'I
hope so.'

My blood starts to boil. Because of Kungu
we have lost our father and uncles. Because of
Kungu father could be dead. But I bite my
tongue till I taste blood, torn between fury and
calming my little brother. Mugo still thinks

that Kungu is a hero.

Finally I hiss, 'No one as angry as Kungu can die.'

But I do not explain. It's safer that Mugo does not know. Only *I* know what Kungu said the night he left for the forest, his words exploding in my mind like British bombs.

THREE

Fury

That night I was sleeping in my father's hut.
Kungu and father were sitting at the hearth.
They thought I was asleep, and so I was until
the thunder and the rain started. And that's
when I heard.

'Two years!' Kungu spat. 'Fighting Japs in
stinking jungles. And what do we get for our
victory? Ordered back to the Reserve so white

men can call me a Kuke and "boy" and expect me to slave on their farms.'

'Hush, Kungu. You'll wake Thuo.'

'But father, our officers lied. They promised us land, but the British Government has given *them* the land. Thousands of acres. And we have scarcely enough to live off.'

Kungu's eyes glinted in the firelight. Then to my horror he tore the kipande pass book* from his neck chain and threw it in the fire.

'This is my country,' he said. 'I won't be treated worse than a white man's dog.

'The British have Britain. Why should they take our land too? How will I or Thuo marry if there is not enough land to keep a family? It will be the end of our Kikuyu people.'

Father sighed, like the wind off God's Mountain. Then he gave his blessing and Kungu walked out into that stormy night,

---

*The employment record that all African males over the age of sixteen had to carry by law.

15

while I huddled under my sheepskin, feeling sick.

My war-hero brother had gone, and I did not have the guts to call goodbye, even though I knew that one of his reasons for leaving was for me.

Not long afterwards, the Home Guard took father and our uncles away for being Mau Mau sympathisers. Then my school was closed and my hopes of becoming a great Kikuyu scholar were dashed. While I herded goats, my hate for Kungu grew. He had killed my future.

Two years on, I am still herding goats, and Mugo is tugging my arm. As I turn to look for our animals, I see smoke rising from my uncle's farm. Then the terrible cry carries across the Reserve: *Uuuu-uuuu-huuuuu*. It is Aunt Mumbi, but the howl seems to come out of my mouth. I forget the goats and run.

FOUR

Exile

'Fire!' Mugo yells. We run down the path as the flames whoosh up Aunt Mumbi's thatched roof. Then our uncles' and cousins' huts go up. I smell petrol, and see brown men in brown uniforms admiring the blaze.

Then a truck comes rumbling down the track and I know. The Home Guards are heading for our farm.

I stop dead, the goats flocking behind me. I turn and start throwing stones at them. 'Yaah, yaah!' Mugo stares as if I'm mad.

'What?' I cry. 'You want Home Guards licking their chops on our goat meat?'

Mugo starts hurling rocks too. Go. Go. GO. Then we run home, yelling, 'Mother, mother. The Home Guards are burning the farms.'

It is no good. What can kids and women do against men with guns and petrol? Mother pulls her cape over her face so she cannot see, but I watch the Guards set fire to our home, raid our granaries, steal our milk cows.

Then they shove us in the truck with Auntie and our cousins and drive us into a wire-fenced compound two miles away. There are many families there, mothers, children, old people, but no men my father's age. They are in detention camps.

Everyone is speechless with shock. They

squat round their pots, pans, hoes, blankets, anything they have managed to carry. While over us looms the Guard Post watchtower.

I try not to shudder. Mugo stares, eyes full of tears.

'Why have they put us in prison?'

I shush him, but inside my heart burns. KUNGU, are you happy now that we're all prisoners?

We sit for hours in the hot sun, wondering what will happen. Then the Kikuyu headman from the Guard Post comes. He says it was Mr Johnson, the District Officer, who ordered the burning of our farms.

He says it is for our own good. My mouth falls open. What?

'You will live inside this new village,' the headman says, pointing to the barbed-wire fence. 'Here we can protect you, and Mau Mau can no longer raid your farms for food. Soon they will be trapped in the forest like wild beasts and killed.'

I turn to look at the forest. It makes no sense. We are much nearer than we were on the farm. Why has the D.O. moved us?

Then I understand. We are bait to catch Mau Mau. I scan the tall trees where the freedom fighters hide. Are you watching us, Kungu?

Then there's no time to think. The headman orders us into the bush to cut timber and thatch to build our huts. Mugo and I go with mother and Aunt Mumbi. They move like sleepwalkers and do not speak.

Who has words for losing a home?

I hack down branches, silently cursing the Home Guards who point rifles in our backs. The British will give these collaborators our land, and I pray to the spirits of our warrior ancestors who live there. *Rise up*, I tell them. *Destroy these thieves and bullies.*

It is a small hope.

When the huts are built, we are forced to dig a great ditch around the village-camp. We dig until our hands are raw. Then sharpened bamboo poles are sunk in the ditch, and the Guards joke, saying the spikes will rip the guts from any Mau Mau who tries to enter.

The digging leaves no time to start new gardens. Instead, the Guards send us out for two hours each day to find food and cut firewood. Mugo and I rush back to the farm to harvest our beans and sweet potatoes.

We bring in the goats and hens to the camp pen, so at least we have some milk and eggs. But soon we find that monkeys have raided our gardens and left nothing to pick.

This time I scream at our ancestors, 'You've abandoned us and I curse you.'

Mugo is so terrified by my sacrilege he sobs all the way back to the camp. I cannot be bothered to comfort him.

As the days pass with less to eat, I feed on hate:

hate for Kungu and the evil he's caused us, for the Home Guards' bullying, for mother's shame at having her basket searched, for the D.O. who burned our home, for the RAF bombers, for the British Army shooting black men.

But secretly, in the dark of our hut, the biggest hatred is for me. Because I am too scared to go into the forest and kill Kungu.

Mother watches me with worried eyes. One day she makes me swear not to run to the forest to join Mau Mau. I almost laugh in her face, 'What me? Your cowardly son?'

Yet, in my dreams, I am always there – trees black as night, creepers coiling like snakes, bombs hurtling on my head, army hunting me down, ground bursting under my feet, the roar of planes and gunfire.

And then one night, as the cold season approaches, I wake from one nightmare into another. Suddenly there is no need to go to the forest. The forest has come for me.

FIVE

Betrayal

Thuuuu-ooo. The sound makes my flesh crawl, like bad spirits. I sit up, staring round the hut where we lads sleep.

'Mugo?'

He is curled under his sheepskin by the hearth and sleeping like a rock. Nearby, our older cousins, Njonjo and Mwaura, are flat out and snoring after twelve hours' ditch digging.

I hug my blanket, listening to the night outside – goats in the pen, an owl hooting. Then I hear it.

'Thuuu-o, for God's sake.'

I spring to the door in terror: damned if I open it, damned if I do not. But it will barely shift. Something that stinks like a dead beast is slumped against it. My fingers grasp the tattered sheepskin caked with mud, the wetness and the cold of him.

Kungu?

My mind spins. A trap? But whose? The Home Guard? Special Branch? Mau Mau? Then I remember the late-night patrol. If I don't hide this stinking heap we are all dead.

I shove the door harder.

'Aaaaah.'

The beast rolls over. I slip outside, listening for the Home Guard. At night their orders are to shoot to kill.

'Kungu. You're hurt?'

'Shot,' the heap breathes. 'Betrayed.'

'But who?'

'No time. Must hide.'

'Not here. You can't. The guards … '

I picture the travelling gibbet that the British send round the Reserve markets to show us what freedom fighting brings. I see the limp man hanging from the noose. I feel the noose around my neck. Bloody Mau Mau!

I want to kick and kick the wretched lump.

'Aaaah!' Kungu gasps. The animal stench pours off him. Then we hear the tramp of boots by the Guard Post. Kungu staggers to his feet.

There's no choice. I drag him inside and lay him on my mat, praying the others won't wake. I hold my breath as the patrol flashlight flicks by the door. I sweat and pray. *Dear God, please let there be no trail of blood. No footprints leading to our door.*

When the boots move off, Kungu grasps my hand.

'You can stop shaking now, little brother.'
There's a dry little laugh that freezes my heart.
'Good thing you did not join the forest army.
We would have had to shoot you.'

My face burns. 'So why come? If you think
I'll betray you?'

He grips my hand till I nearly yell.

'To cut the bullet from my leg.'

'I can't … '

Kungu's grip burns my flesh. 'Stoke the fire,'
he says. 'Put my knife in the flames to clean it.
Hurry.'

My brother yanks the ragged sheepskin from
his thigh. In the firelight I see the congealed,
bloody mess.

I smell his animal smell that almost chokes
me. See his long black hair, lousy and matted
as an unshorn sheep. His boots made from car
tyres.

And I think, *Is this my brother? The once
smart askari who came home from Burma a hero?*

'Bandage,' Kungu says. 'To catch the blood.'

I bring a sack, but I have no bandage.

'Your shirt?'

'No!'

I know he means my school shirt, because I have no other. 'No!'

Kungu frowns.

'I promised mother,' I say. 'Not to go to the forest or help Mau Mau.'

Suddenly I see myself running to the Guard Post, crying that I've caught a terrorist. The British might give back our farm as a reward. Or pay for me to go to Kenya's best high school, as they do for the headman's sons.

My courage soars. I reach for the knife in the hearth.

It will only take a single blow.

SIX

Hideout

Did Kungu read my thoughts? When I look for the knife, he already has it. I jam my fist in my mouth to stop the scream. Kungu is using the red-hot blade to cut the bullet from his leg.

He bites on his filthy cape and makes no sound. Time stands still as I watch this man, and smell his burning flesh.

My hatred dissolves.

This is my brother. My brother.

I stand up and pull the brown paper parcel from the hut rafters. Inside is my school shirt. I rip it into strips for Kungu.

For three nights we hide Kungu in our hut. We lads make him millet gruel, sneak milk from the goats, roast sweet potatoes in our hearth embers.

At first Kungu gets better. At dawn we hide him under our sheepskins, stifling fear through the long day, the Guards' eyes always on us. By night we sit, head to head round the fire, while Kungu whispers stirring tales of how the freedom fighters dodge the British Army across Kenya's highlands.

'We run on the sides of our feet,' he says, 'and leave no prints. Run seventy miles if we have to. Then we thread back tall grasses with twigs to leave no trail.' When Mugo asks about the forest bombing, Kungu laughs his dry little laugh.

'Ha! Those British bomb our hideouts, but not us. The elephants warn us. They go crazy when they hear the planes coming.'

Sometimes we gasp at Kungu's stories. Sometimes we grin like fiends. When he tells how he once tied himself to the top of a forest cedar and brought down a Harvard jet-bomber by shooting its fuel tanks, we bite on our arms to stifle the cheers.

'The RAF never admit such losses,' Kungu says.

But soon I see these are not just warrior tales. Kungu is setting the record straight about his Land and Freedom Army.

'Last July,' he says, 'I raided five settler farms near Lake Naivasha. My men were starving and sick. On the last raid I shot a British farmer. It was him or me. He is the only white civilian I have killed.'

Then Kungu laughs the dead-leaves laugh. 'But I have roasted many white men's cows and sheep.'

For a time we all dream of eating roast meat. Next Kungu says, 'My platoon also raided the Police Post at Nanyuki. We took ammunition, 303 rifles and killed two police askaris. Then early this year we attacked the army camp at Manyenge and killed twenty-three European soldiers and thirty-one African soldiers.

'Last month I executed three of my own men for cowardice, and I shot dead a British police officer who walked into my forest hideout with a bunch of traitor Mau Mau.

'The British call these traitors *pseudo-gangsters*. They are forest fighters who have surrendered to save their necks. Now they spill our tactics to Special Branch. But they haven't found me.

'Not even when I hid in an aardvark hole near this camp, so I could spot my little brothers' hut.'

And finally, after the tales that fire our hearts, Kungu tells us how he was betrayed.

SEVEN

Sky-talker

'Our army has always been scattered,' Kungu says. 'Platoons in Aberdares forests, on God's Mountain, in the Rift Valley. Many miles apart.

'But when the British cut us off from getting food and medicine from the Reserve farms, life in the forest became terrible … '

He pauses as if the memory is too painful.

'That's why some of our leaders approached the British for peace talks. But when I went to the agreed meeting place in the forest and laid down my gun, it was a trap. The army fired on us. Many died. I was lucky to escape … '

'And so now what?' Mwaura asks.

'Back to the forest or hang.' And again Kungu laughs.

That night we all sleep badly.

On the fourth day of hiding Kungu, a military spotter plane flies over. We are out gathering firewood. Someone in the plane shouts at us through a loudspeaker.

Word flies round that it's the English policeman known as Kinyanjui. He is one of the few whites who speaks Kikuyu because he grew up on a settler coffee farm near the Reserve. He says if we don't surrender Mau Mau fugitives, we will be punished.

My insides heave when he says they are after General Kahiga. It is Kungu's forest name.

After the plane goes, Njonjo whispers that he's overheard the Home Guards talking.

'They know Kungu is near,' he hisses. 'Tomorrow the British soldiers will sweep this part of the Reserve.'

That night we sit in our hut, weighed down with fear, expecting the worst. I am stunned when Kungu says, 'I must leave now.'

'But how?' I cry.

This time I am more scared for him than for me. His brow glows with sweat. He still cannot walk properly.

'The way I came. Through the barbed wire.'

'But the ditch. The stakes.'

'I will roll down. Crawl out. Like a cockroach. Have no fear, little brother.'

'But where will you go?'

'A cave I know. I once shared it with a she-leopard.'

I shiver. A window on hell has just swung wide. I see the big cat's yellow eyes, the white fangs. Then I see the falling bombs, hear elephants screaming, the rifles' crack-crack, feel the breath of a pseudo-gangster on my neck.

The words fly from my mouth before I can stop them. But, once said, I cannot take them back.

'I'm coming too.'

EIGHT

Breakout

Now Kungu is the shocked one. 'You? But you're just a schoolboy who promised his mother … '

'Yes,' I snap. 'I did promise her.' Then our eyes meet in the hut's gloom and there is nothing more to say.

I cannot lie and say my fear is gone. It beats on my ribs like swarms of flying ants. I do not know what will become of me, only that the great warrior Kungu will have Thuo at his side.

I slip from the hut before the late-night patrol, listening hard. Only insects call. No sound from the Guard Post. No light on the watchtower. This gives me hope that our plan has worked.

Before the curfew, Njonjo and Mwaura let the Guards find them arguing over a big gourd of millet beer that they had made. The Guards took it of course. Now we pray they are sound asleep.

We must risk it.

I haul Kungu from the hut. He half-walks, half-leans as we creep past our neighbours' huts, across the compound to the ditch. Behind us comes Mugo with a broom, ready to back off fast and sweep away our footprints. Kungu flinches as I help him slide into the ditch.

Watch out for the stakes! Mugo throws me

his sheepskin. I'm carrying a gourd of gruel in a sling, holding a branch to wipe away our footprints on the other side. I slither into the ditch behind Kungu. We edge between the spikes.

It takes a lifetime.

At last I push him up the far side. Then he pulls me up. Then it's through the wire, our sheepskins saving us from the worst barbs.

Beyond the wire, a zone of bare earth surrounds the whole village. It is swept before the night curfew and checked for footprints at dawn. We shuffle backwards. I hold Kungu with one arm, while brushing away our tracks with the other.

The sweat runs down my face like tears. Any second I think the watchtower searchlight will find us. The brushing takes precious time, but if our tracks are found in the morning the whole village will be beaten, or worse.

When at last we reach some cover Kungu

stops dead. I am stunned when he hugs me.

'Go back, Thuo. God go with you. You have proved your courage. I was wrong to taunt you.'

I stand in the darkness, the wire, the ditch, the village-camp all behind me. I think of my mother and the promise I am breaking. I think of my father, maybe dead in Manyani detention camp.

I think of my real home that the Home Guards set on fire. But mostly I smell my brother, the unwashed forest warrior who is fighting for my freedom.

Again I make my choice.

I put my arm round my brother's wasted shoulders, grip him hard. There is nothing but skin and bones beneath the tattered sheepskin.

'Teach me,' I whisper. 'Teach me the forest ways.'

NINE

Forest Flight

So begins the hard trek to the forest. First comes
hail, stabbing like knives. Then as we climb
towards the tree line, lightning splits the sky in
two. For hours we stumble through driving rain,
up to our knees in mud, following secret paths
that only Kungu knows, wading swollen streams.

But finally, as day dawns, the rain turns to
drizzle and fog falls like a shroud. Kungu says

we still have much open ground to cover.
Then he starts shaking like a leaf and I panic,
thinking he is sick.

'Kungu?'

Then I see he is laughing.

'See how God hides us from the British
spotter planes. Come. Soon we'll reach the
high forest.'

He limps ahead, spurred on by some unseen
force. Before my eyes he is changing – no longer
Kungu my wounded brother, but General Kahiga,
warrior leader. Only when we enter the tall trees
does he stop again. He staggers and hugs the
buttress roots of a wild fig that we call mugumo.

'We must pray,' he says. 'Thank God for our
safe arrival.' I hang back. A mugumo tree is
very sacred to our elders, like a church is to
white men.

Kungu smiles, but not unkindly. 'Oh-ho,
Thuo. Still believe the lies those missionaries
told you? That we're nothing but pagan

savages who have no God?'

'It's not that,' I mumble. 'I was baptised at the Mission School. Won't our God mind?'

Kungu sighs. 'Not if your heart is pure.'

So we stand together beneath the fig tree and pray. Then we press on through a twilit world where towering trees shut out the light. Where no birds sing and no buck springs from the underbrush. Where there is only the dripping of leaves, and my feet squelching on muddy game trails.

Once, Kungu stops me dead. Ahead three she-elephants with two calves move silently through a glade. My eyes start out on stalks. I have never seen elephants this close before.

'See,' Kungu hisses. 'Learn from the elephant. They walk always on tiptoe. And if you stay near them, you'll be safe from British soldiers. Elephants smell their shaving cream for miles and keep away.'

My brother teaches me many things that

day. When I trip on a vine and a blue monkey flies barking through the trees, Kungu jabs me in the ribs. 'If a pseudo-gangster hears that, he'll know we're here. Remember that call. It might save your life.'

I blink at Kungu. Our worst garden pests could save my life? The ants flap harder in my chest. The forest closes round, dark and forbidding as my nightmares. Soon it will be night, and Mugo and mother seem far away.

For a second even the village-camp seems like home. Then the cold rain starts again.

Dusk is gathering as we near the leopard's cave. Kungu tells me to check the ground all round for leopard tracks and droppings, but I find none.

'Good,' he says. 'That cave is not big enough for three.'

I stare at the dark hole in the rocky outcrop and want to weep. Is this the refuge we have struggled all day to reach? It looks more like a tomb.

TEN

Alarm!

The cave is scarcely big enough for two. Kungu tells me to block the entrance with boulders. Outside, the rain drips off the trees and fills a crevice, giving us clean water to drink. In the darkness we share some of the cold gruel, and then all night I lie next to my stinking, sweating brother, hoping that mother will forgive me.

But the next day, when I pull back a rock, sunshine spills in. I hear birdsong and my spirits lift. Then I turn and see that Kungu is worse. Sweat beads stand on his brow.

His face is grey. I bathe his head, but he does not wake. I shiver under my sheepskin. The dawn is icy, so I eat a mouthful of gruel and wonder what we'll eat when it runs out.

While Kungu sleeps, I force myself to look at his wound. Blood has soaked the bandages, so I wash them clean, then gather moss from outside the cave and use it to stop the blood, then I bind the leg tighter. I do not know if this is the right thing to do.

Finally I decide to look for the maize stores that Kungu says he has hidden in old tree trunks about the forest. I think of wild honey too. It would be good to eat and would heal Kungu's wound.

I leave General Kahiga wrapped in my sheepskin, take his knife and block up the cave entrance. Then I stand shivering in the morning air, telling myself to watch out for elephant and rhino, to listen for the blue monkey's call. And not lose my way.

The blood pounds in my ears, drowning out the dawn chorus. The ants clamour in my chest. Can farm-boy Thuo survive in this place?

I head into the forest by wading along a stream. I am pleased by my cleverness: no leaving tracks; no getting lost. The icy water laps my thighs and my bare feet slither on cold stones, but I feel more alive than I have for months.

Doves call and finches twitter in the reeds. Everywhere the forest fills my eyes. The tall, tall trees. I gaze round in wonder.

When the blue monkey cries I am so shocked I slip backwards into the stream. As I go under I glimpse a file of ragged black men moving along the bank towards me.

Again the blue monkey cries. Hide!

But where? If I stand up they'll spot me. If I don't, I'll drown. Kungu, what would you do?

The answer comes just in time. A reed. My chest is bursting as I grab for one. I break the base of the stem with my teeth, sucking hard till I can breathe a little air. Then, still under water, I edge under an overhanging bank.

A lifetime passes as I lie in the stream, breathing through my reed straw. I wonder which will kill me first, the freezing water or these men who could be pseudo-gangsters hunting for Kungu.

At last, I dare to poke my nose above the water. Further upstream the men who looked like Kungu are bobbing away into the greenery. I'm about to stand up when again the blue monkey cries, hkaa-hkaa! My heart almost stops.

Good God. One man is still standing by the stream, barely a stone's throw away. He is studying a map. Then he scratches his head like a dog with fleas, tearing the matted locks clean off. I almost swallow the stream.

The hair underneath is short and fair. The face that bends to drink from the stream is painted black.

'Blasted Kukes,' he mutters. 'Blasted Mau Mau baboons. Ruddy wild goose chase.'

A white man. A man from Special Branch dressed up as Mau Mau with his band of traitors – just like the policeman Kungu said he shot?

Now I am so furious I want to yell after his men, 'Shame, you heroes, betraying your comrades to be called baboons behind your backs.'

Instead, I lie in the stream while my blood boils, and that probably saves me. When the coast is clear I run as fast as I can to Kungu, praying to God that they haven't found him.

ELEVEN

Final Mission

They have not found us. Kungu hangs on to life and I fool myself that he's getting better. Day follows day till it grows into one. Yet I am changing. I feel myself grow, like a sapling pushing up to the light.

When there are only berries to eat, rage at the policeman's insults stops my hunger pangs. My senses are sharper too. I can move like a shadow on the dappled trails. I have learned to bear the rain and cold because Kungu says we must not light a fire.

'A spotter plane will see it,' he says, 'then send the bombers. Or a pseudo will smell it.'

Somehow the hardship only hardens my resolve. They will not get Kungu – not the British soldiers, not the pseudo-gangsters.

When Kungu feels better, I help him out of the cave to urinate and do his business. When he raves with fever, I muffle his mouth with my sheepskin. I feed him raw birds' eggs and wild honey soaked in water. When the honey water ferments in the gourd, we become very merry and laugh all night.

And then one afternoon, when I return from foraging, I find Kungu already out of the cave. He is sitting on a fig-tree root, so proud in his sheepskin robes, with his long matted hair.

'Kungu?'

He smiles dreamily. 'Wanted to see the

forest,' he says. 'That cave is so dark.'

'Are you hungry? I've some roots and an eagle's egg.' He shakes his head.

'No, you eat them. No point in wasting them on me.'

Then I see the pool of blood at his feet, and crouch beside him.

'Your wound … '

'Forget it. Sit with me.'

So we sit under the mugumo tree where we Kikuyu speak with God. Sunbeams drop through the tall trees and onto Kungu's ashen cheeks. A blue monkey creeps closer, watching us from the branches. This time he says, 'Peoo, peoo,' as if we are his comrades.

And I know. General Kahiga is dead.

Before darkness falls I find Kungu's matches that he keeps in a waterproof pouch, and light the fire to scare off leopard that might smell his blood. Then I sit by the fire with Kungu. When it crackles, it is as if he is speaking to me.

'Thuo, our people are sick of this war. They are starving to death. Some have lost everything. The British are too clever, turning Kikuyu against Kikuyu. But one day we will have independence.'

Then he makes me promise.

'Thuo, when this war is over, go back to school. Our people will need teachers. It takes great wisdom to learn how to be free.'

And so I promise. But I think, too, of all the things I have learned from Kungu: that there is nothing wrong with feeling afraid, because fear and cowardice are not the same things. It is doing your best that counts.

When the long forest night ends and the laughing doves call, I lift Kungu in my arms. He is cold and stiff and coated in dew, but light as brushwood. I wonder if the British have seen our fire, but it doesn't matter now.

I carry General Kahiga out of the forest where he has fought so long, beneath the camphors and sweet cape chestnuts, through the bamboo thickets and wild fig groves.

I carry him for miles across the Native Reserve. As we go, the sky above the Great Rift Valley turns china blue, and larks call to us from high heaven. There's the smell of crushed mint on the highland air, and the good earth glows red on the cow-tracks and pathways.

Behind, I hear the dead drone of aircraft. We turn to God's Mountain, its snow spires glinting. It is a fine day for bombing. Very fine. We watch the planes bank over the forests. The earth shakes as the bombs fall. *Ker-boom. Ker-boom.*

'Ha!' I say to Kungu. 'You were right. They saw our smoke.'

But we do not care. We are going home, my brother and I. To our father's farm.

I will lay him to rest in the goat pasture overlooking God's Mountain, so that his spirit can join the ancestors and no army sweep will find him.

And I know from now on, in our forest hearts, Kungu and I will never surrender.

The war is done. Now it is time to win the peace.

Author's Note

So how did Kenya become a British colony?

It was the 19th Century discovery of the River Nile's source in Uganda that focused British attention on East Africa. The big fear was that Germany would go to war with Britain, sabotage the Nile source and threaten Britain's trade on the faraway Suez Canal. During the 1880s

'Scramble for Africa', Britain competed with Germany for East African territories, finally taking control of Uganda and neighbouring Kenya, then called British East Africa.

The Lunatic Line

The first objective was to build the Uganda Railway, so troops could be sent to defend the Nile source. Military envoys went to make treaties with the African clans who lived along the line, and a series of small forts was built. Resistance was crushed by military force. But even as the railway was being built (1895-1901) opponents back in Britain were calling it the Lunatic Line. They thought building a 600-mile (966 km) railway across desert, lion country and the Great Rift Valley was idiotic and a waste of money.

European settlement

By the early 1900s the British Government

realised that the railway had to be made to pay. They began to encourage European settlement, and especially by pioneers from the officer and landed classes. It was thought they would instil discipline and have a 'civilising' effect on local Africans. They would also establish large farms that produced cash crops for export.

African lifestyles

When Britain laid claim to East Africa, many different ethnic communities lived there, each occupying their own clan territories. Some were fishermen, some cattle herders, some practised mixed farming, some were hunters. But their territories were not static. Warfare, disease, climate change, failing soil fertility and growing populations all caused people to move.

Farmers like the Kikuyu had been slowly shifting across the continent for centuries. The

Kikuyu clans farmed large estates that included grazing land and garden plots. When fresh ground was needed, the elders bought it from the local hunters. When sons wished to marry, their fathers would give them land so they could support a family. If the clan ever grew short of land, family groups would set out to colonise new territory.

Seeds of conflict

The European settlers rarely considered African culture and beliefs. They had large land holdings and they expected Africans to work as field hands. The colonial administrators tried to protect African interests by creating tribal Reserves. These were large areas, but their boundaries were fixed. They did not take account of growing populations, or the fact that tropical soil erodes once the forest cover is removed.

The Kikuyu also had large herds of cattle

and goats that added to land erosion in the Reserves. These herds were the clans' bank accounts, needed in particular for marriage contracts. The Kikuyu resented it very much when the authorities started ordering herds to be reduced.

The Kikuyu also lived in one of the most desirable parts of East Africa. The soil, though fragile, was very fertile, and the climate good. When the British surveyors marked out the Kikuyu Reserves, they seemed unaware that the Southern Kikuyu had almost been wiped out by smallpox and famine in 1899. The survivors had moved north until they could return to their lands.

When they did return, many found British coffee farmers occupying their gardens and grazing land. To the Kikuyu, land was ancestral land. It had huge spiritual as well as economic importance. Their pleas for compensation were dismissed.

Forced labour

The settlers demanded labour. The colonial administration therefore imposed hut and poll taxes on Africans. These had to be paid in cash, so forcing them to work for the Europeans. Also imposed was a system of chiefs that overrode Africans' own elders' councils. These chiefs worked for the authorities and would round up people to labour on the settler farms. Then in 1915 the passbook or kipande was introduced. Every African male of 16 years upwards had to wear a metal case that held their employment record. They could only leave the Reserves to work for Europeans.

Land shortage

After both world wars the British Government offered large areas of the Rift highlands to European officers under the Soldier Settler Scheme. Yet Africans who survived service in the British forces were not rewarded. Soldiers like Kungu fought in terrible conditions in Burma and for less pay than European soldiers. When they returned home victorious, these brave, highly trained men were seen as a threat.

Their weapons were taken and they were sent back to overcrowded Reserves where they had no future. Those who had received a mission-school education and wished to go to college were refused. The European settlers did not want well-educated Africans. They wanted field hands and clerks. For this reason the Kikuyu tried to set up their own schools and colleges.

The Land and Freedom Army

By the late 1940s all the Africans' grievances were coming to a head. The Kikuyu had run out of legal means to get back all their lost land. Requests to have land title deeds, and a fair say on the Legislative Council that ran Kenya Colony, were refused. When the young

African men and women rallied to the freedom-fighting cause in Kenya's forests, they called themselves 'The Land and Freedom Army'. The origin of the name Mau Mau is unknown, but it was widely used in the media to imply savage tendencies, so disguising the fact that Africans had genuine grievances.

The Emergency

In October 1952 the murder of a senior Kikuyu chief prompted the British Governor of Kenya to call a State of Emergency. The settlers were terrified of African nationalism and wanted the uprising crushed by any means. The colonial authorities then played on Kikuyu clan rivalries and land hunger, and set up the Kikuyu Home Guard to do colonial officers' bidding. Loyal Kikuyu were thus pitted against supposed terrorist sympathisers.

It became a civil war. Kikuyus suspected of supporting Mau Mau were sent without trial to detention camps, where conditions were terrible. Historians have estimated that 100,000 men and women were detained without trial. From 1954, one and a half million civilians were put in village-camps overseen by Home Guards. Thousands died from starvation. Family land was confiscated and used to reward the Home Guards.

Official figures

Many official records from this period were deliberately destroyed. However, a British Government report of 1960 gives the following statistics:

During the Emergency 1,090 Mau Mau were executed and over 11,000 were killed in action.

Mau Mau killed 63 European forces, 3 Asians, 101 African askaris (policemen), and 1,819 loyal African civilians.

32 white settlers were killed.

While all sides committed atrocities, there was no massacre of white civilians, as is often implied. But the extent of the brutality suffered by the Kikuyu people still remains to be discovered.

Independence

The Emergency ended in 1960. Kenya became an independent state in 1963, when Jomo Kenyatta, a Kikuyu leader who had been wrongfully detained for eight years, became the first president. To the settlers' surprise, he offered reconciliation rather than revenge, although many chose to sell up and leave before Independence. The military cost of the Emergency was over £55 million.

For further reading about Kikuyu traditional culture see Jomo Kenyatta's classic account *Facing Mount Kenya*. For more information about the Mau Mau era see *Mau Mau Warrior* by Abiodun Aloa.